# The Adventures of

# Allie the Alewife

By Barbara Brennessel

Illustrated by Marisa Picariello

We thank Friends of Herring River and the Wellfleet Cultural Council for financial support. And a special thank you to Alice Iacuessa, and Nina Picariello for their thoughtful suggestions.

ISBN – 13:   978-1508778660
ISBN – 10:  1508778663

Allie the alewife spent the summer in Pleasant Pond.

Each day she watched the kayakers glide over her head.

Allie swam with the children as they took their swimming lessons. She watched them jump off the dock and practice their strokes.

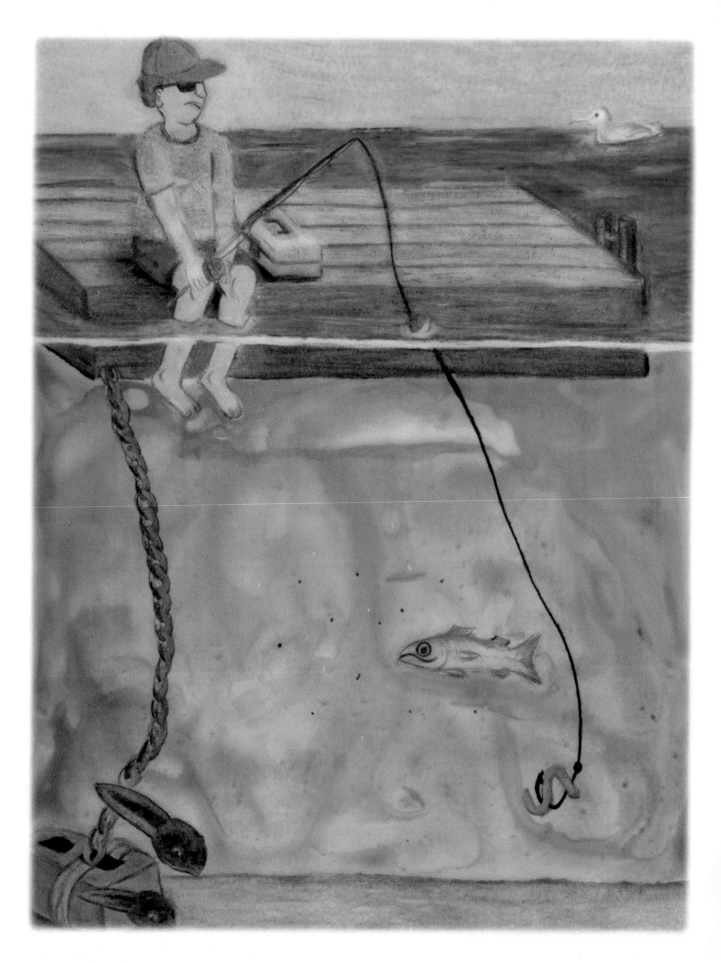

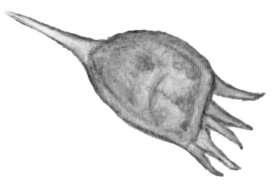

The boys and girls who fished with worms could not catch Allie because she did not eat worms.

She ate zooplankton: tiny, tiny creatures in the water that she filtered through her gills.

All summer long, there were plenty of zooplankton in Pleasant Pond.

When summer ended, the water became colder.

The dock was gone.

The children were gone.

Zooplankton were harder for Allie to find.

Allie wondered what she should do. But then, she met some other small alewives.

Together they formed a school and practiced their synchronized swimming.

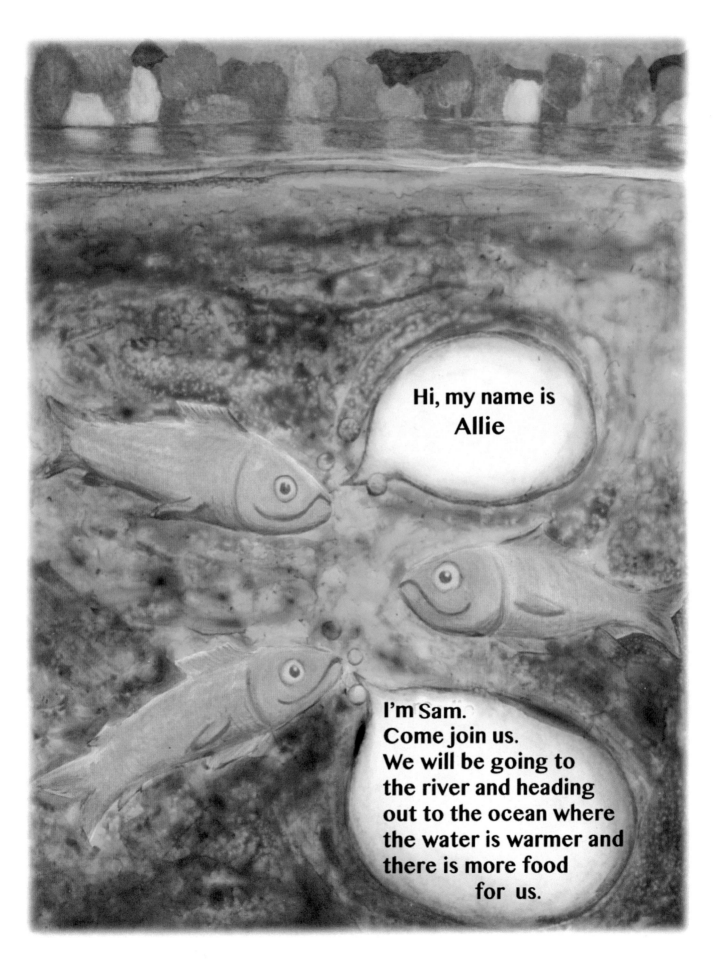

Back and forth, around and around the little fish swam.

The school was getting ready to leave the pond and travel to the river, which would lead them to the ocean.

They would be in the nursery school class called "young of the year."

After it rained and rained, the river filled with water and the current was fast. The rushing water gave the alewives a quick ride downstream.

But to their surprise, there was an old dam across the river. The only way the fish could keep going was to tumble over it.

Luckily, they landed safely under the crashing water.

Allie and her friends had never been this far from Pleasant Pond.

Soon they reached the estuary, where the fresh water of the river starts to mix with the ocean water and becomes salty.

As time went on, the young of the year grew bigger and bigger, and swam farther from the estuary.

Still in tight formation, the young fish eventually reached the open ocean and joined other alewife nursery schools.

Together they avoided dangers such as being eaten by bigger fish, like cod.

The alewives also stayed away from large fishing boats, called trawlers, which could scoop them up with their big nets.

After spending three years in the ocean, Allie and her schoolmates had grown to full size.

When spring arrived, around the time the forsythia was in bloom, the alewives sensed that they should leave the ocean.

Swimming along the coast, they searched for the familiar place where they were born.

Finally the school reached their estuary.

Here, they spent some time getting used to the water which was not as salty as the ocean.

Sam became their "scout." He would help to find the way back to Pleasant Pond.

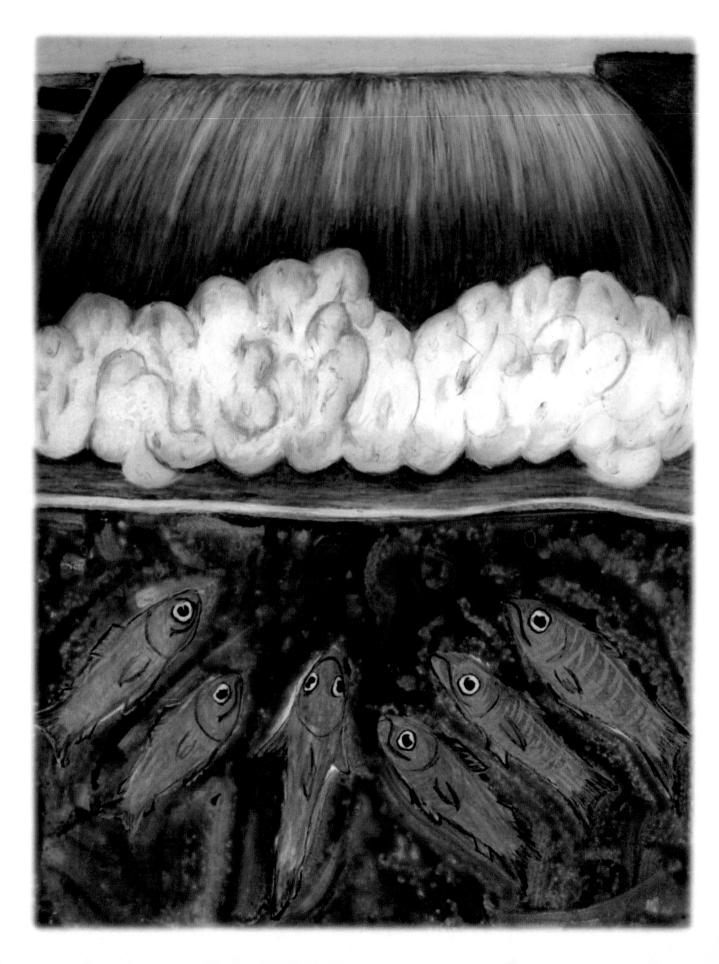

When conditions were right, Sam led the way up the river.

The rest of the school followed him upstream against the current.

Soon, the alewives arrived at the old dam and didn't know what to do.

Luckily, Sam discovered a way over the dam. It was a fish ladder.

It had many steps, but also some places to rest.

Up they went, following his lead.

Swimming up the ladder was hard work!

Allie and the alewives were tired and hungry but they kept swimming upstream, avoiding raccoons, otters, snapping turtles, and birds that were looking for a fishy meal.

The school swam by some people who were counting each of the alewives as they passed upstream.

Along the way, the fish also met baby eels called elvers, who were heading to Pleasant Pond, too.

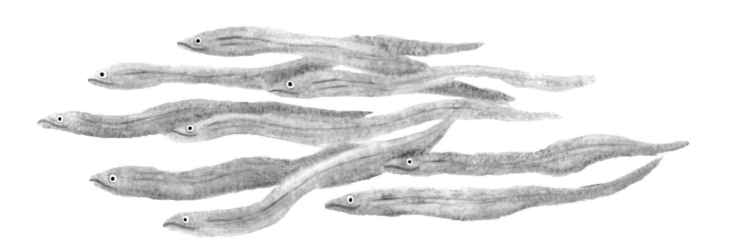

Finally, Allie and her alewife friends sensed that they were in a familiar place. They had made it back home to Pleasant Pond, where they were born.

Now it was time for them to have babies of their own.

The new babies spent a wonderful summer in Pleasant Pond, just like Allie and her friends when they were young.

The tiny fish swam with the children as they took their swimming lessons, and watched kayakers glide overhead.

The summer passed and the babies became the new "young of the year."

At the end of summer, the young fish also made the trip from Pleasant Pond to the ocean.

When they were three years old, it was their turn to travel back to Pleasant Pond with the other alewives.

Each year the alewives faced the difficult swim up the ladder.

One year they had a surprise. The dam was gone! The people who counted them had removed it.

Without the dam, it was much easier to swim up and down the river, between the ocean and the pond.

It would be clear sailing from now on.

RIVER RESTORATION PROJECT
IN PROGRESS

SUPPORTED BY
THE FRIENDS OF
THE RIVER

Barbara Brennessel is a biologist who recently retired from teaching at Wheaton College in Norton, MA. She is a board member of Friends of Herring River in Wellfleet, MA.

Marisa Picariello graduated from Wheaton College where she studied art. She is now living in Wellfleet, MA. Her work can be seen at: www.marisapicariello.net

Made in the USA
Middletown, DE
09 March 2022

62380621R00022